BENJI FRANKLIN
KID ZILLIONAIRE

a Capstone company — publishers for children

Raintree is an imprint of Capstone Global
Library Limited, a company incorporated in England
and Wales having its registered office at 7 Pilgrim Street,
London, EC4V 6LB – Registered company number: 6695582

www.raintree.co.uk
myorders@raintree.co.uk

ISBN: 978 1 4747 0732 9

19 18 17 16 15
10 9 8 7 6 5 4 3 2 1

British Library Cataloguing in Publication Data
A full catalogue record for this book is available
from the British Library.

Printed and bound in China.

BENJI FRANKLIN

KID ZILLIONAIRE

BUILDING WEALTH

(and Superpowered Rockets!)

written by
Raymond Bean

illustrated by
Matthew Vimislik

Contents

Introduction 6

CHAPTER 1
Asteroids! 8

CHAPTER 2
Big trouble 16

CHAPTER 3
Spacing out 24

CHAPTER 4
Travelling in style 31

CHAPTER 5
Up, up and away 38

CHAPTER 6
The asteroid net 45

CHAPTER 7
Suit up! 54

CHAPTER 8
Zero gravity 65

CHAPTER 9
Nice catch! 70

CHAPTER 10
Bright future 78

Introduction

My name's Benji Franklin! After inventing a best-selling computer app that helps people come up with creative and time-saving excuses, I became the world's youngest and, well, only ZILLIONAIRE!

But I quickly discovered that life wasn't all about the money. I've decided to use my newly found wealth for the greater good - such as saving the world from cloned killer dinosaurs, building super-powered rocket ships and launching a solid gold submarine. Or two!

Here's a few people you should know:

DAD: He likes building one-of-a-kind inventions, and he spends a lot of time tinkering in our workshop. His latest projects include an orbiting surveillance satellite and magnetic suits that can rescue drowning fishermen and sailors. Plus, he's always excited about my ideas!

MUM: She's always putting other people before herself. She is a regular volunteer at the food bank and taught me that helping others is important, rewarding and fun. She also runs a farm (which I bought her).

PROFESSOR SNOW: He knows everything there is to know about cloning, climate change, nano-bots and anything else that can easily turn into a catastrophe. I recently helped him to save the world from Troodon dinosaurs!

That's about it.

Okay, time to save the world ... again!

CHAPTER 1

Asteroids!

One morning, I was out in the workshop downloading data from the satellite. Dad was working on his magnetic suits. He'd reversed the magnets and his safety system seemed about ready for a real-life trial. He knew a fisherman in town who had agreed to try it out with his crew. He'd dropped his boat off at our workshop earlier in the morning, and Dad was installing the system in the boat.

That's when I saw it…

An asteroid appeared on the satellite's data system. It was on course to collide with Earth!

"You might want to take a look at this, Dad," I said, my heart pounding.

He was working on the boat, twisting at something with his spanner. "I can't right now, Benji. Is it good news or bad?" he asked.

"Both," I said.

"Well, does it look like something's going to take out our satellite?" he asked.

"Well, no, and that's part of the good news," I told him. "The bad news … this might take out the planet. The WHOLE planet!!"

My dad is extremely organized. Everything he owns has a place, and he always puts things where they belong. I thought it was funny that even though there was an asteroid screaming towards the planet, the first thing he did was put his spanner carefully back in his toolbox. If there was a time to simply drop it on the floor and be sloppy, this was it!

"What's the other good news?" asked Dad.

"Maybe we can stop it," I said.

"Benji, this asteroid is rushing towards Earth at incredible speed. I don't think we can do anything," he said, sceptically.

"From my calculations, the asteroid is still sixty days from impact," I explained.

"Then I wouldn't panic just yet," he said. "I've seen space debris that looked like it was on course for impact suddenly change direction and sail right on by. Now, it's getting late. You need to get to the bus stop."

Huh?!? How can he expect me to go to school after what I just told him? "I don't think you heard me when I screamed, 'the WHOLE planet'," I said. "I need to track this asteroid and send the data to someone who can help save us! Then maybe I can buy a laser canon … or a super-sized missile launcher … or a titanium fly swatter the size of a football pitch, or –"

"Benji, you're twelve years old," he said. "The world can survive without you on this one. You're not the only person with a satellite tracking this thing. Everything will be fine."

Obviously, I didn't agree, but I could tell there was no way Dad was going to let me stay at home.

* * *

On the way to school, all I could think about was the asteroid. I was working on my smartphone, which was really hard to do with the bus bouncing and all the kids talking. I made a list of the ways to destroy, or send off course, an asteroid:

HOW TO STOP THE ASTEROID

1. **Blow to bits.**
2. **Send off course with megatonne explosion.**
3. **Redirect course with giant sail.**
4. **Break to pieces with high-tech machines.**
5. **Create a chemical reaction to disintegrate.**

I was so focused on my list that I didn't notice the person sitting next to me. Cindy Meyers. "You know, you're not allowed to use your smartphone on the bus," she said. "Do you think that just because your app is so popular you can do whatever you want?"

I rolled my eyes. "Good morning to you, too, Cindy," I said, trying to be polite. "I'm busy on an important project. It's not as though I'm playing video games or texting like you."

"I'm not texting or talking on my phone because that would be against school rules," she whined.

"I'll be watching," I said, getting back to work.

"That makes two of us," she warned. "It's going to be a real shame when the headmistress takes your smartphone away and bans you from the bus."

"If you knew what I was working on you wouldn't be giving me a hard time," I said.

She laughed. "I find that hard to believe."

Cindy had always been difficult, but she was being especially annoying today.

"What's your problem?" I asked.

"I don't have a problem," she said. "You're the one who thinks you're so cool ever since you created that ridiculous Excuse Yourself app."

"Who said I think I'm cool?" I said. "For your information, I've never considered myself cool."

"Well, that's not how it seems. You created that app, and then you didn't even have to come to school because you're a big deal now. You weren't the only one who worked hard on that app project," she said.

She was upset that her app didn't get as much attention as mine. I couldn't even remember what her app did! "I haven't been to school because I was busy helping out the food bank," I explained.

"I think you're a troublemaker," she said.

"Then why did you sit next to me?" I asked. I had bigger things to think about than Cindy.

"Because I'm on the School Decency Committee and you're on my radar," Cindy explained. "You haven't been around to see the damage your app created. Kids are making up all kinds of excuses for things thanks to your reckless idea."

I got a little anxious because I had barely been to school since I created the app. I knew that loads of people had downloaded it, but I hadn't had any time to see how kids were using it.

"Well," I began, "I'm about to see for myself."

CHAPTER 2
Big trouble

Everything seemed pretty normal when I got to school. My app wasn't causing any problems as far as I could see. I was definitely getting more attention than usual, though. More people seemed to know my name, which was funny because before the app I wasn't exactly popular.

On my way to my first lesson, a few kids patted me on the back. I didn't like all the attention. It was a little stressful. I found myself walking quicker than usual. I slipped into my seat in the classroom, relieved to be out of the corridor.

The teacher started the lesson by welcoming me back to school. The class erupted with applause. "You're a superstar these days," she said. "We've been following your success online. I can't believe how huge your app, Excuse Yourself, has become."

I'd been so busy with the Troodon dinosaurs and Prof. Snow that I hadn't had time to read what was being said about the app.

"I'm pretty shocked myself," I said. "Honestly, I haven't been able to follow what's going on with the app because I've been working."

"I thought you were away because of the app," Mrs Heart said.

"Actually, I was busy with another project for my mum's food bank," I explained. "The headmistress gave me permission to take a few days to work on it. Remember?"

"That's not an excuse, is it?" Mrs Heart joked.

"No, but maybe I should add it to the app," I said with a smile.

"Are you rich?" said someone at the back of the classroom.

"It's not polite to ask a question like that," said Mrs Heart. "We're all very happy for you though, Benji."

Realizing that everyone at school knew I had made a LOT of money was a bit embarrassing. James, the kid sitting next to me, leaned over and whispered, "How much do you actually have?"

"I don't know," I said, which was basically the truth because the number was always changing. I'd checked the total before school, but there were too many zeros to count!

I'd only been away from school for a week, but it felt like a year.

* * *

When I got home later that day, I went straight to the workshop. Dad was at the computer and looked as though he'd been there all day.

"Benji, I was wrong," he said. "People don't seem to be tracking this thing. You've found something that others haven't noticed yet. I can see why! It's not a known asteroid. I've been searching the database all day and can't find any record of it."

"What does that mean?" I asked.

"We might be the only ones who know it's there," he exclaimed. "Most satellites are designed to locate asteroids larger than a kilometre. My satellite is great at detecting asteroids *smaller* than a kilometre. This one is about the size of a twenty-storey building, so it's much harder to locate than a larger one."

I did the sums in my head. A storey of a building is about four metres. If the asteroid was twenty storeys, it measured about eighty metres long!

"That's small?" I asked.

"Compared to some larger asteroids," said Dad. "It's big enough to cause a lot of damage, but still small enough to go undetected. The good news is it won't destroy the planet, but if it hits Earth it will do some real damage."

"Shouldn't we call someone or notify the government?" I asked.

"Not yet," he said. "Let's give it a few days and see if the asteroid changes course. We have some time."

I logged on to my computer to research the kind of damage an asteroid could do if it hit Earth. I learned that the asteroid that caused the extinction of the dinosaurs was about ten kilometres wide.

The asteroid I had found wasn't even close to the size of that one, but it was large enough to flatten buildings for eight kilometres from the site of impact.

I worked to try and calculate the date of impact. I knew Dad was doing the same thing.

ASTEROIDS

Space rock!

My asteroid!!

Dino killer!!!

Neither one of us said anything for about an hour. Then, I broke the silence.

"If my calculations are correct," I said. "The asteroid will hit Earth on Mum's birthday!"

I didn't have the heart to tell Mum that the world could be blasted by an asteroid on her birthday. When I went to the farm later that night, I didn't say anything about it.

Mum hadn't wasted any time taking over the farm I'd recently bought for her. It was already producing milk and eggs, and she had a full-time staff. She had also bought a few refrigerated vans for deliveries. That night, she was checking on the chickens, as I walked over to her.

"You've been on your computer too long again," she said. "Your eyes are all bloodshot."

"No more than usual," I said.

She stopped and took another look at me. "What's on your mind, Benji? You look worried."

"I'm fine, Mum. Today was my first day back at school. It was a bit strange. Kids are really interested in the app and all the money I'm making." I said this knowing it was true, but that my real concern was the asteroid.

"Children your age don't normally experience this kind of success," she said. "It's natural for your friends to be interested and to ask a lot of questions."

"I suppose," I replied.

"There's something else that you're not telling me," she said. "What is it?"

I couldn't lie to my mother. "Our satellite located an asteroid this morning. It's on track to crash into Earth in about a month."

"I know. Your father told me a few hours ago," she said, walking ahead of me.

"WHAT?! Why didn't you tell me that?"

"I wanted to see if you'd tell me on your own. Why didn't you tell me?" she said.

"I didn't want to worry you," I explained.

"I'm not worried, Benji."

"You should be!" I exclaimed. "It's on a collision course with the planet. The WHOLE planet!"

"You'll work something out," she said.

Mothers. They're always so supportive. But this problem was a little out of my league.

"I bet you already have a solution brewing inside that head, and you don't even know it yet," she said. "You don't want an asteroid ruining your mother's birthday, do you?"

CHAPTER 3
Spacing out

I went for a walk on the footpaths behind the farm. I couldn't help feeling that a Troodon dinosaur was going to jump out at me from behind a tree.

It was pretty unbelievable when I stopped to think about how much things had changed in such a short time. It was hard to even remember a time before Excuse Yourself.

As I walked, I imagined scenarios that might change the course of the asteroid or destroy it. I'd read online once that if you blow up the asteroid it becomes a group of small asteroids instead of one big one. The group of smaller ones acts like a shotgun blast and can cause even more damage!

My mind kept going over all of the scenarios I'd listed on my computer. There simply had to be a solution.

Instead of blowing up the asteroid, what if there was a way to capture it? I wondered. I could land some sort of remote-controlled unit on it and then fly it like a spaceship.

I tripped on a large stone and stopped to pick it up. I held it in my hands for a while wondering how I could stop it if it were hurtling through space at thousands of kilometres per hour.

I threw it as hard as I could and watched it sail into the woods. I picked up another stone and hurled it in the same direction. A vision of a net wrapping around the stone came to me.

A net would stop or slow the stone down, but I couldn't work out how to get a large net into space. Even if I did, could I change the course of an asteroid?

I picked up another stone, and my phone rang.

"Hi, Dad," I answered.

"Hello, Benji," he said. "I just spoke to Prof. Snow. He has someone he'd like you to meet."

"The Troodon didn't escape again, did they?" I asked, hoping that wasn't the case.

"Nope, the dinos are safe and sound," Dad said. "This is about the asteroid. Why don't you ask Mum to drive you home? We need to talk."

* * *

When I got home, Dad was sifting through old aeroplane parts in the back field. "What's up?" I asked.

He climbed out from the rusty cockpit of a small plane and sat on the wing. "Come on over," he said, dusting off a place for me to sit.

"What are you doing?" I asked.

"I'm looking for spare parts to see if I can make another low-orbit rocket," he said, "but I wanted you to come home to talk about Prof. Snow."

"What did he say?" I asked.

"He asked for my permission to give our number to another scientist," he explained.

"Why?" I asked.

"He said that a very prominent scientist contacted him for help, and he suggested you."

"What did you say?"

"That between the Troodon and Excuse Yourself you've been busy," said Dad. "It might be good to take a little break."

"I'm fine, Dad, really," I assured him. "I can handle it."

Just then, my phone rang.

"Hello," I said.

From the other side, in an English accent, a man's voice said, "Hello, Benjamin. My name is Sir Robert Dransling. You come highly recommended by Prof. Snow."

"That was fast," I said.

"There's no time to waste," he replied. "A situation has come to my attention in the past twenty-four hours that causes me great concern. If my information is correct, you've noticed this – ahem – problem as well."

"You mean the asteroid?" I asked.

"SHHHHH!" he said. "Someone might hear you. If people find out that there's an asteroid on a collision course with Earth, there will be a mad panic. Discretion is the best course, lad. We mustn't breathe a word of this to anyone else."

I looked around at the back field, the rusty plane and Dad. "My lips are sealed," I said.

"I'll send for you tomorrow," he said. "I'm flying you out to New Mexico so that we can talk in person."

"But I have school tomorrow –"

"I'll see you tomorrow, Mr Franklin. There's not a moment to waste." Then he hung up.

"He wants me in New Mexico tomorrow," I said.

"But you have school," said Dad, "and I'm doing my first test of the magnetic system out at sea."

"We'll work something out," I told Dad.

"Who was that man anyway?" he asked.

"He said his name was Sir Robert Dransling," I replied.

"Sir Robert Dransling?!" Dad exclaimed. "He's a world leader in space technology. They say he'll be the first person to provide space flights to tourists as a holiday!"

Really? I thought. *Maybe he can help me with my space station zoo idea!*

CHAPTER 4
Travelling in style

I went to school the next day, as usual. During my maths lesson, the teacher receieved a message. She told me to go to the office because I was going home early.

Mrs Petty, the headmistress, and her secretary both looked confused.

"Benji, your father called and asked if you could leave early," Mrs Petty said.

I looked around the room. "Who's picking me up?" I asked.

The secretary pointed outside. Through the window, I could see a long black limousine parked in front of the school. Its windows were tinted, and there was a tiny British flag painted on the passenger door.

"What's that?" I asked.

"We were hoping you could tell us," said the headmistress. "It's highly unusual for a child to be picked up by a non-family member."

"Who's in the limo?" I asked.

"Your father wouldn't say," she told me. "He just said that he was out at sea and your mother was away on business for the food bank and that a car had been sent to pick you up."

"Alright then," I said. "I'm free to go?"

"Yes, I hope everything is okay," Mrs Petty said.

When she said, "I hope everything is okay," I realized that she thought something was wrong. Based on her expression, she probably thought someone in my family had died or something.

"Everything is fine," I said.

"Keep up that positive attitude," Mrs Petty said.

When I walked out, a man stepped out of the driver's seat and opened the back door. I realized that all the classrooms facing the front of the building were full of kids pressed up against the windows.

"Good morning, Mr Franklin," the chauffeur said in a British accent.

"Nice car," I said. I wasn't sure what else to say to him. My heart was racing pretty fast.

"I realize this is highly unusual," he said. "However, we are in the midst of a decidedly unusual situation. Your father is returning from the fishing vessel he's on, and asked us to pick you up in order to save time. I have your mother waiting on a video call."

He held out his phone, and I could see Mum on the screen. "Hi, Benji," she said. "I've already left the house and your father is on the boat. Sir Robert sent this car for you. It's going to take you to meet Dad at the dock, and then you're off."

"Off to where?" I asked.

"Your father has all the details," she said. "I wish I could come along, but I'm halfway to Shiny Desert to make my delivery."

"Okay, Mum," I said. "Does this mean I'll be off school for a few days?"

"I don't know, honey," she said.

The chauffeur nodded his head to indicate that I would in fact be away for a few days. I gave him a thumbs up.

"You've already missed too many days," said Mum. "I don't want you missing too much more. But this seems like the opportunity of a lifetime, and your dad will be with you the whole time. Have fun, and give me a call later to let me know how things are going."

* * *

During the journey to pick up Dad, the driver kept the glass partition between the front seat and the back of the limo shut. It was a little strange sitting alone in the back of that huge car. I ate a bag of crisps and watched some television.

I may have to buy one of these, I thought. *And maybe one for Mum, too. Then she wouldn't have to drive herself to places like Shiny Desert all alone.*

Dad hopped in when we reached the docks. He was wearing one of his magnetic suits.

"How's the suit working?" I asked.

"Really well," he said. "But we've only tested it in calm water. I'll have to increase the magnetic force on the boat for it to work properly in rough seas."

I was wondering how long it was going to take Dad to acknowledge that I was taking time off school. And that we were being driven in a limo by a complete stranger.

"Sounds great," I said. "Anything else going on?"

"Not really," he replied.

I watched him looking at the TV for a while until he finally snapped out of it. "What's happening? Where are we going?" he asked.

"Are you going to wear that magnetic suit the whole time?" I said.

Dad quickly unscrewed his helmet. "Where are we going, Benji?"

"I thought you knew," I said.

The glass partition between the front and back seat suddenly slid down. The chauffeur glanced towards us in the mirror. "We're driving to the airport," he said.

"But where are we going?" I said.

"The desert," he told us.

"Desert?" cried Dad. "Which one? Besides, I'm not dressed for the desert!"

The glass partition smoothly slid upwards and cut us off again from the driver.

"How many deserts are there in New Mexico?" I asked.

For the rest of the journey, Dad told me all about Sir Robert Dransling. He sounded like an extremely successful man. He owned newspapers, shipping companies, TV stations, radio stations and a lot of technology businesses. He'd even been knighted!

Why did he need me?

CHAPTER 5

Up, up and away

We drove up to a special gate at the airport. Security guards opened it, and we turned right onto the runway. It was a special section of the airport for all the private jets.

"Wow!" Dad said. He's been interested in planes ever since he was a kid.

I lowered the partition between the driver and us. "Are we going on one of these jets?" I asked.

"The one at the end," he said.

At the end of all the amazing jets was the coolest one of all. It looked like a bullet with wings.

"That's the ECS Bolt 41," Dad said.

"I see you know your aircraft," the driver said. "But that's actually the ECS Bolt 42. It's *next* year's model. No one else has anything like it."

"It looks like half plane, half spaceship," I said.

"You could say that. Ah, we are here," he said, stopping the car. He climbed out and politely opened my door.

Dad and I stepped out.

A long staircase slowly lowered from the plane. A man stood at the top. He waved.

"That's Sir Robert Dransling," whispered Dad.

Sir Robert was really tanned, as though he'd been in the sun every day of his life. He wore a lab coat over a smart business suit.

He shook my hand. "Mr Franklin, please do come aboard and make yourself at home," he said.

I'd been on a plane two other times in my life: once to Florida and once to California. On both of those trips, we flew on a normal plane.

This plane was like something from a film.

The luxury aircraft looked like an expensive hotel. There were actual rooms. It had a living room, kitchen and even a few bedrooms.

"Can I offer you gentlemen something to eat?" asked Sir Robert.

"We'd love a few turkey sandwiches, if it's not too much trouble," Dad said. "I've been out on the water all morning, and Benjamin hasn't had a chance to eat lunch yet."

Sir Robert pressed a button on his phone. "Done," he said. "They will be ready in a few minutes."

"That's pretty cool," I said.

"I agree," he said. "It's very cool. From what I hear about you, young Benjamin, you could buy a plane like this of your own."

"Maybe I will," I said.

"I didn't make my first million until I was twenty-five," said Sir Robert. "From what I understand, you're only twelve, and you're already beyond that."

"Benjamin hasn't had a lot of time to really think about the money he's made," my dad explained. "He's been busy working for Prof. Snow since the app was released."

"I've also been helping my mother establish a small farm for the food bank she runs," I added.

"Intelligent, modest and giving. You may just be my new favourite person, young Benji," Sir Robert said.

Just then, a waiter handed me a plate with a turkey sandwich and a glass of fruit juice.

"And you may be mine," I said, smiling and raising my glass.

"I can offer you much more than a simple sandwich, Benji," said Sir Robert. "I contacted you because I know that you have a low-orbit satellite collecting data on space debris. I have several of my own in orbit. My team and I first spotted the asteroid a few days ago. I realized that you and I were probably the only two people with satellites designed to identify an asteroid of that size."

"It was very good of you to invite us here," I said. "But what exactly can we do for you?"

"It's what I think we may be able to accomplish together," he replied. "My focus in life is on helping others to reach their full potential. I'm sure my team could work out some way to deflect or destroy this asteroid, but I'm more interested in what *you* would do with it, Benji."

"Seeing as you're so wealthy, don't you have access to the world's best scientists?" I asked. "Why are you asking me?"

"Indeed I do have access to the world's brightest and best," he said. "However, as I've already pointed out, you seem to be the only other person to have spotted the asteroid. If the 'world's best scientists' haven't even been able to locate the asteroid, why would I want their help in trying to destroy it?"

I thought about what he said for a moment. It was amazing that no one else had detected an asteroid that could possibly flatten towns and cities if nothing was done to change its course.

"The reason I asked you here is that I believe you're an extraordinary young man," Sir Robert continued. "I told Prof. Snow that having those Troodon was going to become a problem. What surprised me was when he told me that a twelve-year-old solved the problem for him. I'd like to know what you'd do to solve this asteroid situation."

"I have an idea," I said. "I wouldn't blow it up, I'd try to land it."

"I'm listening," he said.

"It'll be expensive," I said.

"Too expensive for a couple of zillionaires like us?" he said, smiling.

"Never," I said. "Have you ever heard of graphene?"

CHAPTER 6

The asteroid net

Of course Sir Robert had heard of graphene. It's only the most exciting new material on the planet. It's incredibly thin and light, but graphene is also the strongest material known to man.

A few years ago, two scientists won the Nobel Prize for their work with graphene. They say it's so strong that a piece of graphene as thin as cling film is strong enough to hold an elephant!

"We've done some work with graphene at my facility. An incredible material," Sir Robert said.

"Is it as amazing as people say?" I asked.

"It's flexible, incredibly strong and can conduct electricity," he said. "It's a miracle material."

Dad and I knew all about graphene. We'd read articles and watched a lot of videos about it. Still, we'd never actually seen it up close.

"Do you have graphene at your facility now?" Dad asked.

"We do," Sir Robert replied. "We plan to use it a great deal in the future, in everything from mobile phones to aeroplanes. But the technology isn't very advanced yet."

"Do you think a giant sheet of it would be strong enough to catch an asteroid?" I asked.

"It's definitely strong enough to catch the asteroid without breaking," he said. "But it would be almost impossible to predict where the asteroid will impact Earth. The odds of placing the graphene in the right place are a million-to-one."

"I'm not talking about catching the asteroid on Earth," I explained. "I'm talking about catching it in space before it enters the atmosphere. You could use one of your spaceships to get the graphene up there."

Sir Robert stood up and walked over to a large thin computer screen on the wall. He clicked the controls a few times and opened what looked like an animation program. "Benji, come over here," he said. "Let's see if we can get a sense of exactly what you're talking about."

Dad and I walked over to the screen.

"Tell the computer what you're thinking," said Sir Robert. "The program will create a visual model."

"You're joking!" I exclaimed.

"You're not the only person capable of creating a cool computer program, Benji," he said. "If you describe your idea to this program, it will show us what the concept will look like. Give it a go."

"Okay." I had the idea formed in my head, but it was tricky explaining it to the computer program clearly enough so that it could create a visual model for us. "We launch a rocket into space containing a graphene mesh long enough and wide enough to catch the asteroid," I began.

The screen immediately displayed an animation of a rocket deploying a long thin mesh in space.

I continued. "Four other rockets would then attach themselves to each corner of the mesh. These rockets would be able to hover in space, holding each corner of the sheet in place to capture the asteroid as it zooms towards Earth."

The high-tech machine took a few seconds, but the screen created an animation similar to the images I had imagined.

"This program is absolutely amazing!" I said.

"Much cooler than a turkey sandwich?" Sir Robert joked.

"Let's hear the rest of your idea, Benji," Dad said. "Don't lose your concentration."

"Well, when the asteroid makes contact with the mesh, the four rockets will fire," I said. "This will allow us to remotely lower the asteroid to Earth safely. And I know the perfect place to land it."

I couldn't believe that in just a few minutes the program had managed to create what I was seeing in my mind. I had worried that the plan was a little far-fetched, but seeing it there on the screen, I felt it was possible.

"Begin production of materials," Sir Robert told the program.

"What will that do?" I asked.

"It will send the plans to my team, and they can get to work on it right away."

"That's astonishing," Dad said.

"It's technology, Mr Franklin."

"I love it," I said.

"You haven't seen anything yet," Sir Robert said.

* * *

We touched down about three hours later at his facility in the desert. The place looked like a scene from *Star Wars*. There were several buildings built around what looked like a futuristic airport.

People worked busily everywhere I looked.

He had more jets, racing cars and rockets than I could have imagined. Many of them looked like rockets that had been used a long time ago. "I'm a bit of a collector," he said.

The luxury aircraft came to a stop, and we climbed out and onto the runway. He and Dad talked about the early days of aviation as he gave us a tour of his facility. I could tell that Dad was having the time of his life. As the sun was setting Sir Robert said, "I'd like to show you gentlemen my most important project. Follow me."

We walked to a large building on the far side of the runway. It was buzzing with activity. There were people in bright red suits assembling what looked like spacecraft.

"This is the future, Benji," said Sir Robert. "You're looking at my prized possession. It's the next step in aviation and the craft that will lead humanity into space in large numbers."

I couldn't believe what I was seeing. It was the most advanced rocket ship I'd ever seen, and I'd seen them all online before.

"This is a top-secret machine," he continued. "Every part you see is made right here at the space centre. I don't take any chances on getting a poor product or on other people learning what I'm up to. I hope I can count on you two to help keep my secret."

"Of course," Dad said.

"I'm just trying to work out what it can do," I said, looking at the scene in front of me. This wasn't a sci-fi film. This was the real thing!

"These are low-orbit ships," explained Sir Robert. "Their missions will be programmed ahead of time and no pilots will be needed. All you do is open the door, get in and off you go into the great beyond. Space tourists will get into low orbit, take a few pictures, film some video and basically have the time of their lives."

"It's the coolest idea I've ever heard!" I said.

"We have several ships completed and ready to go. I was just waiting for the right time to test them. We'll use your asteroid plan as the reason to launch them into space."

CHAPTER 7
Suit up!

That night, Mum called to see how things were going and to check if I'd be going to school the next day. Dad told her that the things I was experiencing were too extraordinary to miss and I would probably be away for a few days.

After dinner, one of Sir Robert's assistants showed Dad and I to a small building at the edge of the airport. "You gentlemen will be staying here for the next few days, so make yourselves comfortable," he said. "Please let me know if you need anything."

He gave us each a laptop that accessed my data from Dad's satellite and gave us access to all of Sir Robert's data, too. His satellites were so much more advanced than the one Dad had launched. They even had live video feeds from space.

Dad and I were up half the night looking through the satellite data. We must have fallen asleep really late because the next thing I knew, it was morning. I was drooling on the sofa and Dad was snoring on the floor.

There was a knock at the front door. It was Sir Robert. He came in and sat next to me on the sofa. "I see that you two are settling in."

"We spent most of the night exploring your satellites," Dad said. "They're really fantastic!"

"That's kind of you to say, but I'm just as amazed that you used scrap parts to get something up into orbit that functions as a satellite," he said to Dad.

"You haven't seen what we've got on our land," I said. "It's not your average scrap heap. It's like a storage yard full of everything you can imagine. Dad's been messing around with mechanical things for so long he can build anything."

"I'm just a hobby builder," Dad said.

"My own father was the same way," Dad added. "He once built me a hovercraft out of a paddling pool, a microwave oven and an electric toothbrush."

"That's absolutely amazing!" Sir Robert said.

"Yeah," said Dad. "It didn't go very far, but it was a lot of fun."

"I grew up in private schools," Sir Robert said. "I've always been academically gifted, but I've never been very hands on. It's good for me to spend this time with you both. You're true inventors in the purest sense."

"And *you're* a super inventor," I told him. "This place is like Disneyland."

"I'm happy to share it with you," he replied, smiling. "We have a busy day planned, but I thought we could have a little fun before we roll up our sleeves and get to work."

"Can we fly in one of your ships?" I asked.

"There's no better time than the present."

The ship he showed us could carry two to four passengers. Sir Robert pressed a button on the outside of the ship and three seats popped up. They were large, comfortable-looking and sat next to each other in an arc.

The ship was like a large toy. It had small wings on each side. It looked as though it could be part of a ride at an amusement park. I couldn't believe this little thing would be able to carry us into outer space.

"Can it really take us into outer orbit?" I asked.

"It's more than capable. In fact, I think you'll be surprised at how easily the Day Tripper can take us on a round trip. Are you gents ready for your first taste of space?"

Dad looked as though he was about to pop with excitement. If he were a kid he'd be jumping up and down. "I'm ready," Dad said. "I've been ready for this moment since I was a child."

"Me too," I said sarcastically.

"Benji, when your father and I were children people thought that we'd be able to visit space in our lifetime. But technology didn't deliver it fast enough for me. That's why I decided to create the technology I wanted on my own terms."

"Have you been up before?" I asked.

"This will be my tenth trip up. Only a handful of people have been up so far. I'm proud to inform you that you'll be the first, uh, non-adult I put into space."

A man came up to us with a trolley containing three folded-up spacesuits. "Here are the suits you requested, Sir Robert."

58

"Thank you, Arthur. We'll be off in about ten minutes. Please alert the team and the tower."

"Will do, Sir."

Before I knew it, Dad was sat on the floor and had his suit half on. "Well, I'm thrilled to see you're so excited," Sir Robert said. "Let's suit up and get going!"

Moments later, we were sat in the ship. It really did feel like an amusement park ride. When the engine turned on, it wasn't as loud as I'd expected.

I sat in the middle seat between Dad and Sir Robert. The control panel was really simple. I'd expected it to be full of gadgets and gizmos, but it wasn't. There were cameras showing us a view of the rear and each side of the craft. There was a touch screen in front of each seat giving data such as time, temperature, speed and so on.

There were several interactive touch tabs: tower comm, video, email, notes, music and GPS.

That was it. The inside of the ship was simple, clean and really modern. There was even a cup holder. I wondered if it really kept drinks in place or if they simply flew around the ship once it reached zero gravity.

Ah, zero G!! I'd always wanted to go to space, and I'm sure the view is amazing, but the real reason I'd always wanted to go to space was to experience weightlessness.

"Sir Robert, will we be able to experience zero gravity in the ship?" I asked.

"Of course!" he said. "What would a trip to outer space be without experiencing zero gravity?"

"But, the cockpit ceiling is so low and the area we're sitting in is so tight," Dad said. "I don't understand."

"Trust me. You'll experience zero gravity."

We all buckled up and the ship pulled slowly out of the hangar.

It was a perfect day; there wasn't a cloud in the sky. We rolled along the runway, picking up speed. In twenty seconds, the front tipped up and the ship took flight. It was amazing how safe I felt.

We slowly gained altitude. Before I knew it, we were above the clouds. "How are you both feeling?" Sir Robert asked.

"Fantastic," I said. "I can't believe we don't need helmets or anything."

"I'm so used to seeing astronauts in heavy gear," Dad added.

"That was one of my main aims with this little ship," said Sir Robert. "I wanted the passengers to feel like they were in a car."

"Or an X-wing fighter!" I said.

"Go ahead and recline if you'd like. The button is on the side of your seat. When we get into outer orbit you may want to lay your seat back completely to get a better look at the stars."

"I'm fine," I said, feeling my first bit of nervousness. I didn't want to admit that I was worried, but all of a sudden I was getting more and more nervous.

The numbers showing our altitude were climbing so fast I couldn't read them, and the speed was picking up pretty dramatically. We were climbing quickly. I knew that in a matter of minutes we'd either be in outer space or in a million pieces!

I thought about Mum and how she'd be worried out of her mind if she knew what Dad and I were doing. "Can I call my mum once we're out of Earth's orbit?" I asked.

"Of course. You can call her whenever you like," Sir Robert said. I relaxed a little and couldn't wait to get high enough to see Earth as a blue ball floating in space.

The ship climbed and climbed until I could feel a difference. The engine cut off and the ship seemed to float.

"Did you know that once you've reached an altitude of eighty kilometres above the planet you are, by definition, an astronaut?" Sir Robert asked.

I looked at the touch screen and we were at ninety-nine kilometres and counting.

"Welcome to space, gentlemen," he said.

It was such a strange sensation looking back on the planet. It was just as I'd seen it in videos and pictures, but it was real.

Dad literally had a tear in his eye.

For a split second, I felt like I might cry (or throw up!). It was overwhelming.

I was in outer space!

CHAPTER 8
Zero gravity

"Hi, Mum, I'm in space. What are you doing?"

"What do you mean you're in space? Where's your father?" she asked.

"I'm right here," Dad said leaning over so she could see his face.

"You're joking, right?"

"I'm happy to report, madam, that your two men are officially astronauts and are safely orbiting Earth as we speak."

"What are you doing in space!"

"It's fine, Mum. It's the most amazing thing I've ever seen. Sir Robert's ship is so comfortable you wouldn't even believe it's a spaceship."

"I wish you had called to let me know before deciding to blast off."

"It all happened so fast," Dad said. "It seemed like the opportunity of a lifetime."

"I'll have them safely back on the ground in less than twenty minutes, Mrs Franklin."

"Alright, but you call me the second you're back on Earth!" Mum insisted.

"Roger that," I said, hanging up.

"You were wondering about zero gravity," Sir Robert reminded me. "Press the button on your touch pad."

A clickable button appeared on my touch pad that read Zero Gravity. I pressed the button and immediately the glass cover above our heads rose up. It stretched up about five metres before stopping.

Sir Robert unbuckled his harness and rolled forwards into zero gravity. "Feel free to unbuckle when you're ready."

"Let's go!" Dad said enthusiastically.

I clicked the button on my harness and immediately felt weightless. Rather than stay in my seat as I would have on Earth, I gently floated out. I reached out to grab something to balance myself and ended up grabbing Dad's ankle. Sir Robert was already a couple of metres above us and doing somersaults. I noticed a pen fall out of his pocket and float in the air near him.

I pushed off Dad's ankle and propelled up towards the ceiling of the ship. I tucked my knees up to my chest and rotated over in a flip. "This is the absolute best thing ever! We've got to get Mum up here one day," I said.

"You can email her a video of the entire flight. The ship records everything," Sir Robert said.

"Can I have a copy?" I asked.

"If your plan to capture the asteroid works, you can have more than that," he said.

For the first time since I had climbed into the ship, I thought about the real reason we'd come to the desert. We were there to help capture an asteroid. It was time to return to Earth and get to work. Sir Robert clicked a button and the ceiling started lowering back to its original size. We all buckled back in and began our descent to Earth. I took one last look at the planet from space.

"Soak it up, Benji," Dad said. "You may never get an opportunity to visit space again."

"I'm quite certain this is the first of many space flights for young Mr Franklin," Sir Robert said.

"I hope you're right," I said.

"Trust me," he said. "You'll be back."

CHAPTER 9

Nice catch!

It was a good thing that we got an early start on all the preparations because the asteroid was travelling faster than we originally thought. After about a week of people working around the clock at the facility we were ready to put my plan into action. Dad and I stayed in New Mexico for the whole week. Because we were working, Mum decided to stay and help out in Shiny Desert until we were ready to go home.

Dad, Sir Robert and I went back into space in one of his ships before the rockets were launched. One of his teams stayed at the facility and another prepared the landing spot for the asteroid. Once we were in space Sir Robert handed me the digital screen that controlled the rockets. "The moment of truth has arrived, Benji."

I took a deep breath. There was so much adrenaline rushing through my body I felt I might burst. "What if this doesn't work?" I asked.

"What if it does?" he said.

"It will be the most amazing thing ever," I said.

"Then let's do the most amazing thing ever!"

Dad patted me on the back. "Let's do it. It's time to put things in motion."

On my screen I had a view of the asteroid. It was approaching exactly as we'd estimated. I clicked the button to launch the first four rockets. The video from the ground showed all four firing and launching. I waited a few seconds and clicked to launch the fifth rocket containing the graphene mesh. It blasted off exactly as planned.

"Phase one complete," Sir Robert said.

We watched the video screens from each rocket and the coordinates of where they were headed. Within minutes, they were in place.

They were each programmed to carry out the mission, but if anything went wrong, I had the ability to override the program from our ship.

The fifth rocket released the graphene mesh and cut its engines as planned. The other four moved into position. Each one docked into a corner of the mesh, spreading it out like a gigantic space web. We zoomed closer in our ship for a visual inspection of the set-up. I felt like I was dreaming. There I was in space about to catch an asteroid!

"Is this really happening?" I asked Dad as we circled the mesh.

"It is really happening," Dad said. "Don't ask me how, but it's happening!"

"We better move to a safer distance," Sir Robert said. "This is all going to happen very fast."

We travelled for a while until we all agreed we were safely away from the asteroid. We tracked its every move on the video screen.

It was moving so fast I started to feel concerned that it would destroy the mesh and crash to Earth. I held my breath for what seemed like forever as it approached.

Closer … closer…

It made a direct hit at the centre of the mesh, which ignited all four rockets. The force of the rockets pulled in the opposite direction that the asteroid was travelling. We worried that the force of the asteroid would tear the mesh away from the rockets, but the graphene was strong enough to hold on. It stretched out a lot, and kept stretching!

The force of the rockets slowed the asteroid dramatically. The force of the asteroid's speed and the force of the rockets created an epic tug-of-war battle. Which would win?

Within a few minutes it was over and the asteroid was gliding safely under the control of the rockets. "Phase two complete," Sir Robert said sounding relieved.

Dad didn't say a word. He was sweating pretty heavily. I noticed that his fingers were crossed. "Are you alright, Dad?" I asked.

"About as good as I can be under the circumstances."

Phase three of the plan was the part I was looking forward to the most. The rockets carefully guided the asteroid down towards Earth. We followed behind. We were close enough to watch it with our own eyes. The asteroid was so much bigger than I'd imagined. It was like a floating mountain!

I couldn't believe how well the rockets were working. At the pace they were going we'd be on the surface in a matter of minutes.

"You should probably call Mum," Dad said.

He was right.

I clicked the screen and dialed Mum. Her face appeared on the screen. "Hi, Mum! What are you doing?"

"I'm working. We just got back to Shiny Desert a little while ago. I made another trip back to the farm to pick up more supplies for the town."

"Great! Do me a favour. Go outside and look up in the sky."

"Benji, I'm pretty busy. We've got a load of supplies that we need to organize."

"Trust me. I'll see you in a few minutes." Then I hung up.

"Phase four coming up," Dad said.

"Phase four on the way," I said. We were getting low enough that I could see the ground. We were under the clouds. Things were coming into view.

"There," Dad said. "There's Mum's truck."

I saw the truck and spotted Mum. She had walked out of a building and was looking up at us. I could only imagine what was going through her mind gazing up at a massive asteroid supported by four rockets.

People from the nearby town were pouring out of the buildings too. There was a real commotion.

The rockets safely landed the asteroid on the exact coordinates we'd programmed. It was the perfect spot just outside the town.

The ground vibrated when the space rock made contact. Sir Robert landed our ship near the asteroid and Mum ran over to meet us.

CHAPTER 10
Bright future

By the time the team had sprayed down the asteroid with water and it was cooled to a safe level, hundreds of people had lined up for a look. Sir Robert's team handed him a microphone.

"Citizens of Shiny Desert," he began. "We at Dransling Industries realize that you've fallen on hard times. You're a hard-working community. You don't deserve the misfortune that fell upon you when Techron left you without jobs. I wasn't familiar with your story until a young friend of mine brought it to my attention. Through a series of miraculous events we've managed to save the planet from a deadly asteroid *and* your town all at once."

"Please accept this asteroid as a gift. It should provide adequate income as a tourist destination for many years to come."

"Additionally," continued Sir Robert, "I plan to move a portion of my business here to your town. I'm building my space tourism business, and I'm opening an assembly plant right here in Shiny Desert. Construction of the new plant will begin as soon as possible and we will begin recruitment tomorrow. We look forward to a bright future together!"

The crowd cheered.

"This was all your idea, wasn't it?" Mum asked.

I smiled and gave a small nod.

"I don't know what to say," Mum said. "Benji, you managed to solve the town's problems and save the planet in one swoop. You're my very own hero!"

I was a bit overwhelmed by it all. It had been a crazy couple of weeks. I knew my life would never be the same again, but I also knew I didn't want to change too much.

That's when I heard Sir Robert say, "Ladies and gentlemen, I can't stand up here and take all the credit for today. There's a young man who was the brains behind this whole thing. He's here somewhere…"

"He's talking about you, Benji," Mum said. "Get ready to go up on the stage."

I took Mum by the hand and quickly led her out of the crowd. "What are we doing?" Mum asked.

"The hero never sticks around for a thank you," I reminded her. "Besides, I have something I want to show you."

I led Mum over to the ship. "Look at this!" I said.

"Benji, this is very pretty, but we should be getting back."

"I'd rather show you something else," I said.

Dad ran up to us. "I lost you both back there. Benji, Sir Robert is looking for you."

"Let him take the credit. I'd rather take Mum for a spin."

"Great idea," Dad said. He opened the door. "After you, my dear."

"Where are we going?" Mum asked.

"Trust me," I said. We all climbed in. I called Sir Robert's phone. His face appeared on the screen. "Benji, where are you? These people want to thank you."

"You enjoy it. I'm going to take my mum for a spin if that's all right with you."

"By all means. Just don't forget to come and pick me up when you're finished."

"Will do," I said. I hung up and told Mum to get ready.

"Benji, do you know how to control this thing?"

"I don't need to. It's already programmed."

"Programmed to go where?"

"To space," I said, pressing the launch button. The ship lifted off the ground. Mum cried out and grabbed onto Dad.

"Will I like it?" she asked, looking terrified.

"You'll love it," I said, and the ship bolted up towards outer space.

Mum let out another cry, and then she said, "Benji, you're too much! What on Earth are you going to accomplish next!"

"I have no idea," I said. "But I can't wait to find out!"

NEO
(near earth object)

NOTICE OF PAYMENT

FROM:
Benjamin "Benji" Franklin

TO:
NEO (Near Earth Object)

ITEM:	QUANTITY:	AMOUNT:
Liquid Fuelled Rockets	5	$8,000,000
Graphene Sheeting	49,000 m²	$1,500,000
Liquid Jet Fuel	1	$235,000
Tills	2	$450
One-Storey Building	1	$654,550

TOTAL COST: $10,390,000

PAYMENT DUE UPON RECEIPT

PAID!

Cha-Ching!!

RAYMOND BEAN

Raymond Bean is a successful author of children's fiction. He writes for children who claim they don't like reading.

Raymond is a teacher with fifteen years of classroom experience. He lives with his wife and two children in New York, USA.

Glossary

access obtain or retrieve; opportunity to approach someone

adequate just enough, or good enough

adrenaline chemical that your body produces when you need more energy or when you sense danger

chauffeur person who is employed to drive a car for somebody else

collision crash in which two or more objects hit each other

coordinates numbers used to show the position of a point on a map, graph or line

discretion behaviour that avoids revealing confidential information

remotely from a distance

scenario outline of a series of events that may happen in particular situations

sceptical doubting that something is really true

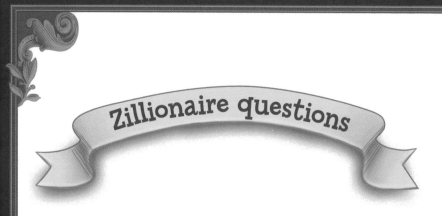

1. Benji missed a lot of school to help Sir Robert. Do you think it was worth it? Is there a way that Benji could have kept his commitment to school AND solved the asteroid problem?

2. Benji comes up with several ideas to save Earth from the asteroid. Do you think he chose the best solution? Try and think of some other solutions, and decide which one you believe would work best if an asteroid really was about to hit Earth.

3. Do you think that Sir Robert could have come up with a solution to stop the asteroid from hitting Earth on his own? Why do you think he asked for Benji's help?

4. Identify a problem that you've noticed in your home or classroom. Perhaps your doorbell at home doesn't work, or one of your classmates always mistakes your lunch box for hers. Now think like Benji! What can you do to solve this problem? What will you need?

5. Benji knows his mum is trying to help the town of Shiny Desert, so he lands the asteroid there to be utilized as a tourist attraction and bring money to the town. Write a chapter that continues the story after the end of this book. What happens in Shiny Desert? Does Benji's plan work?

6. When they land the asteroid successfully, Benji doesn't want the attention of the crowd. Write about a time when you succeeded at something. Were you embarassed by the attention it brought you?

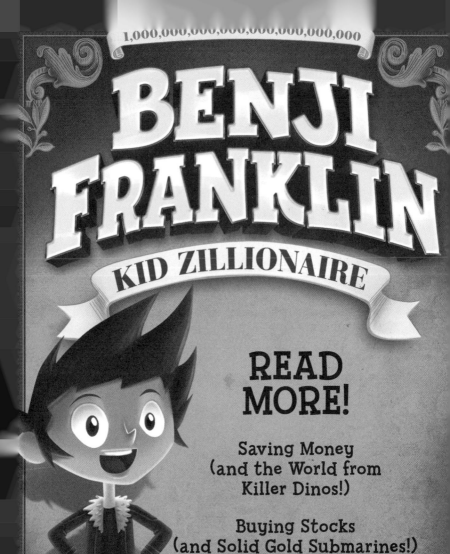

1,000,000,000,000,000,000,000,000

BENJI FRANKLIN

KID ZILLIONAIRE

READ MORE!

Saving Money
(and the World from
Killer Dinos!)

Buying Stocks
(and Solid Gold Submarines!)

Investing Well
(In Supersonic Spaceships!)